This is a Genuine Vireo Book

A Vireo Book | Rare Bird Books
453 South Spring Street, Suite 302
Los Angeles, CA 90013
rarebirdbooks.com

Copyright © 2019 by Neil Cohen

FIRST HARDCOVER ORIGINAL EDITION

For more information, address:
A Vireo Book | Rare Bird Books Subsidiary Rights Department,
453 South Spring Street, Suite 302,
Los Angeles, CA 90013.

Illustrations by Neil Cohen

Set in Casual
Printed in China

10 9 8 7 6 5 4 3 2 1

Publisher's Cataloging-in-Publication Data available upon request.

SAVE THE WENT WORTH!

by Neil Cohen

Liberty Tower,
New York

Municipal Building
New York

Bankers Trust Co.   Building
New York

Singer Building,
New York

Times Building

DEDICATED TO

APRIL SILVER

Liberty Tower,
New York

THE STORY OF ONE
BUILDING and its GARGOYLES and A MAN

WENT WORTH

NOT SO LONG AGO, ON MOST BUILDINGS THERE WERE STATUES, FACES, DECORATIONS, DESIGNS, COLUMNS, GARGOYLES AND GNOMES. THEY MADE ALL THEIR BUILD-INGS LOOK STRONG, BOLD, AND FUNNY. UP ON THE FAMOUS WENTWORTH BUILDING, ANYONE COULD SEE...

"ROCKY"

A CARVED STONE STATUE OF A **FOOTBALL PLAYER** WHO ALWAYS BRAGGED ABOUT HOW BIG AND STRONG HE WAS, AND HOW MUCH HE LIKED TO LEAD A TEAM TO VIC TORY!

NOTHING SCARES ME

ROCKY

RIGHT BESIDE HIM WAS
"LIZZIE"
WHO WAS PART RABBIT, PART BAT, PART
LIZARD, PART SQUIRREL, AND PART CAT...
AND SINCE SHE WAS PART EVERYTHING...
SHE WAS SMART!!!

AND OF COURSE
THERE WAS
TAXI, THE PIGEON
WHO LIKED TO
SIT ON
ROCKY'S
HEAD

ROCKY DID NOT LIKE WHEN TAXI SAT ON HIS HEAD, BUT TAXI WAS AN OLD FRIEND AND THERE WAS NOTHING HE COULD DO.

THEY ALL LIVED ON THE FAMOUS WENTWORTH BUILDING...

ONCE, THE WENTWORTH BUILDING WAS THE BIGGEST AND MOST FUN BUILDING IN THE CITY,

AND EVERYBODY LOVED IT.

One day a man named MISTER DONALD HAIRDOUX announced:

I havE BIG plans for that old Wentworth Building

HISTORICAL NOTE:
No one in the city listened because no one in the city even remembered the Wentworth Building.

MISTER DONALD HAIRDOUX'S PLAN WAS THAT
HE WANTED TO TURN THE
WENTWORTH BUILDING
INTO
ONE GIANT MIRROR...

I'm Loving this idea!

...since he liked to look at himself all day, he
thought that EVERYONE would want A BIG GIANT MIRROR.

ONE BY ONE
ROCKY AND HIS
FRIENDS WERE
TAKEN OFF
THE BUILDING

AND CHEERY AND DREARY BROKE IN HALF

AND AS MISTER H DROVE THEM TO A JUNKYARD,
TO ALL THE GARGOYLES
SOMETHING BECAME VERY CLEAR...

EVERYTHING FAMOUS HAD ONE!!

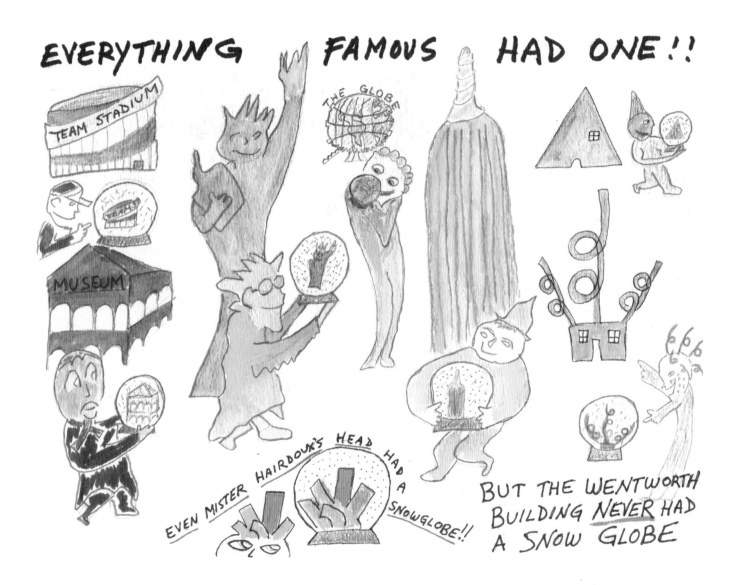

EVEN MISTER HAIRDOUX'S HEAD HAD A SNOWGLOBE!!

BUT THE WENTWORTH BUILDING NEVER HAD A SNOW GLOBE

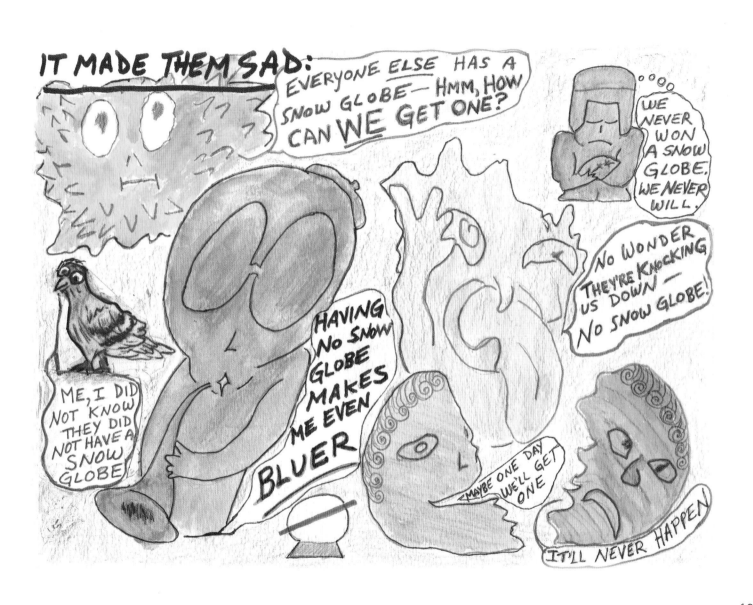

WITHOUT A SNOW GLOBE TO MAKE THEM FAMOUS, THEY KNEW THAT MISTER HAIRDOUX COULD KNOCK DOWN THEIR HOME.

THEY LOOKED TO BIG BRAVE ROCKY TO COME UP WITH A PLAN TO SAVE THE WENTWORTH! — BUT HE JUST LOOKED SCARED. THEY WONDERED WHY. THEN...

I WAS SUPPOSED TO BE CARVED INTO A MAN MAKING BREAD...

... BUT THE STONE CARVER GOT DISTRACTED AND LOOKED THE OTHER WAY, AND...

HE BROKE MY HAT!!

SO, TO FIX THE MISTAKE...

THEY TURNED MY BROKEN HAT INTO A HELMET

AND PUT STITCHES ON MY BREAD TO MAKE IT A FOOTBALL!!!

SO YOU SEE...

24

I NEVER WAS A FOOTBALL HERO BECAUSE
I WAS NEVER SUPPOSED TO BE A FOOTBALL
PLAYER.

AFTER ALL THAT DRAMA, LIZZIE NEEDED TO TAKE A DEEP BREATH.

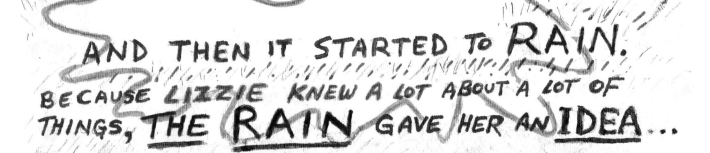

AND THEN IT STARTED TO RAIN. BECAUSE LIZZIE KNEW A LOT ABOUT A LOT OF THINGS, THE RAIN GAVE HER AN IDEA...

"IT'S A WAY TO SAVE THE WENTWORTH" SAID LIZZIE. "LET'S GET OUT OF HERE AND WE'LL TRY IT—FOLLOW ME!"

SHE FOUND AN OLD SEE-SAW AND THEY MADE THEIR ESCAPE...

LET'S GET Rowdy!!!

Oh Yeah

HIT IT!

JUNK YARD

YOU'RE NEXT, ROCKY

AMERICAN SEE-SAW MADE IN USA 1951

SOFT MUD

WHILE EVERYONE ELSE ROLLED DOWN THE HILL, LIZZIE LEADING THE WAY, BEHIND. SCARED ROCKY STAYED HE WAS STILL AND EMBARRASSED.

AS IT KEPT RAINING HARDER, LIZZIE EXPLAINED TO THE OTHERS HER VERY SIMPLE PLAN...

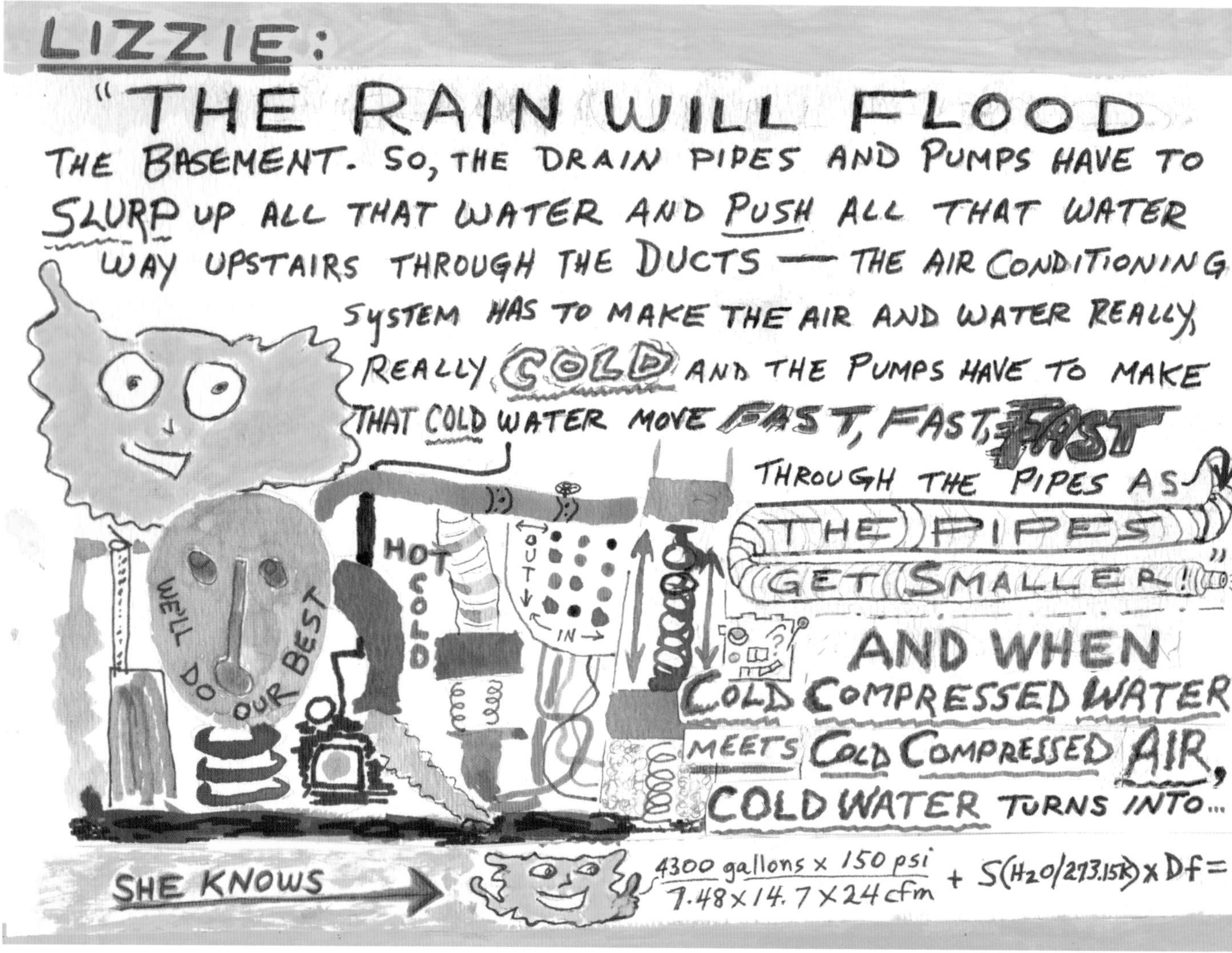
LIZZIE:
"THE RAIN WILL FLOOD
THE BASEMENT. SO, THE DRAIN PIPES AND PUMPS HAVE TO
SLURP UP ALL THAT WATER AND PUSH ALL THAT WATER
WAY UPSTAIRS THROUGH THE DUCTS — THE AIR CONDITIONING
SYSTEM HAS TO MAKE THE AIR AND WATER REALLY,
REALLY COLD AND THE PUMPS HAVE TO MAKE
THAT COLD WATER MOVE FAST, FAST, FAST
THROUGH THE PIPES AS
THE PIPES
GET SMALLER!"
WE'LL DO OUR BEST
HOT
COLD
OUT
IN
AND WHEN
COLD COMPRESSED WATER
MEETS COLD COMPRESSED AIR,
COLD WATER TURNS INTO...
SHE KNOWS
4300 gallons x 150 psi / 7.48 x 14.7 x 24 cfm + S(H2O/273.15K) x Df =

... THE RAIN STOPPED...

AND ON THE **HOTTEST** SUMMER DAY OF THE YEAR...

SNOW CAME OUT OF ALL THE PIPES CONNECTING THE BUILDING'S **FACES,** GARGOYLES, AND **STATUES**!!!

—AND—

THE ONCE-FORGOTTEN WENTWORTH (WHICH NEVER HAD A SNOW GLOBE) SUDDENLY BECAME...

THE WORLD'S BIGGEST SNOWGLOBE!

EVERYONE NOW REMEMBERED THEIR OLD FRIEND THE WENTWORTH BUILDING →

IT WAS **SNOWING** <u>IN</u> **SUMMER** AND EVERYONE CAME OUT TO PLAY!!!

WENTWORTH

AND ONE WOULD <u>THINK</u> <u>THIS</u> WOULD BE OUR "BIG HAPPY ENDING." BUT <u>NO</u>; <u>BECAUSE</u>... →

ROCKY, WHO WAS STANDING ON THE THE HILL THAT WAS NOW COVERED IN ICY SNOW, WISHED HE COULD SAVE THE BUILDING. BUT HE WAS JUST A BIG CARVED ROCK!

HOW COULD ROCKY HELP?

WHAT COULD HE DO?

THEN ROCKY REMEMBERED

HIS GOOD OLD FRIEND!

(THE PIGEON)

Pigeonus Uberus →

Rocky

CALLED OUT TO TAXI THE PIGEON, WHO LANDED ON ROCKY'S HEAD, WHICH MADE ROCKY SLIDE DOWN THE ICY HILL

MISTER HAIRDOUX REACHED OUT FOR THE SWITCH TO KNOCK DOWN THE BUILDING, BUT...

THE WHOLE CITY CHEERED!!

THE WENTWORTH BUILDING GOT ITS VERY OWN SNOW GLOBE

THE WENTWORTH

MY FAVORITE PLACE IN THE CITY!

WRITER + ILLUSTRATOR NEIL Cohen FROM QUEENS, N.Y.
IS THE CO-WRITER CO-DIRECTOR OF "CHIEF ZABU,"
THE CULT COMEDY. HE NOW LIVES IN SANTA MONICA
AND THE HUDSON VALLEY.